THIS WALKER BOOK BELONGS TO:

_____

_____

_____

For my father

First published 2001 by Walker Books Ltd
87 Vauxhall Walk, London SE11 5HJ

This edition published 2004

10 9 8 7 6 5 4 3 2 1

Illustrations © 2001, 2004 Russell Ayto

The right of Russell Ayto to be identified as illustrator
of this work has been asserted by him in accordance
with the Copyright, Designs and Patents Act 1988

This book has been typeset in Beniolo

Printed in China

British Library Cataloguing in Publication Data:
a catalogue record for this book is available
from the British Library

ISBN 1-84428-468-9

www.walkerbooks.co.uk

THE OTHER DAY I MET A BEAR

A Traditional Tale

illustrated by

Russell Ayto

WALKER BOOKS
AND SUBSIDIARIES
LONDON · BOSTON · SYDNEY · AUCKLAND

The other day I met a bear

out in the woods, away out there.

He looked at me. I looked at him.

He sized up me.   I sized up him.

He said to me, "Why don't you run?
I see you don't have any gun."

I said to him, "That's a good idea.

Come on now, feet, get out of here!"

And so I ran away from there,

but right behind me ...

came

And then **I** saw ahead of me

a great big tree. **Oh**, glory be!

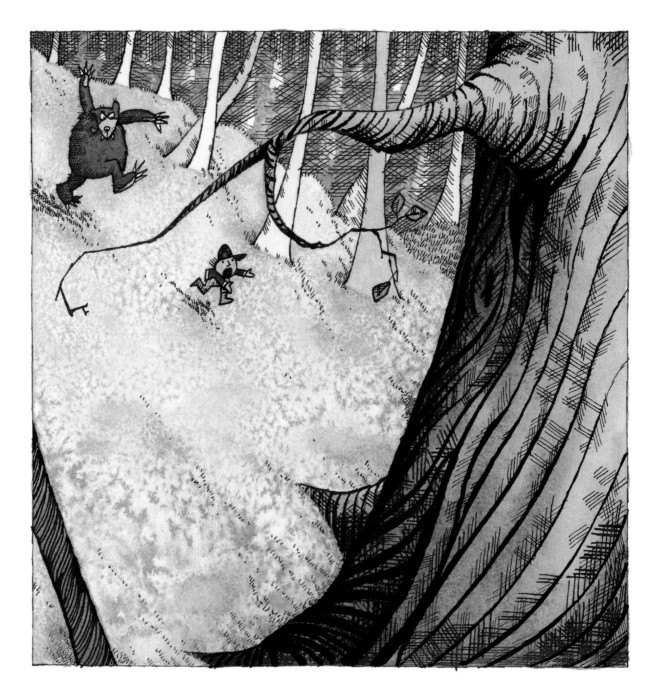

The lowest branch was ten feet up.

I'd have to jump and trust my luck!

And so **I** jumped

into the air ...

but missed the branch

away up there.

But don't you fret and don't you frown -

I caught that branch on the way down!

That's all there is. There ain't no more.

Unless . . .

WALKER BOOKS is the world's leading
independent publisher of children's books.
Working with the best authors and illustrators
we create books for all ages, from babies
to teenagers – books your child will
grow up with and always remember. So…

FOR THE BEST CHILDREN'S BOOKS,
LOOK FOR THE BEAR